Norwood and Tux®

And The Magic Mittens

Norwood and Tux®

Printed in the United States of America

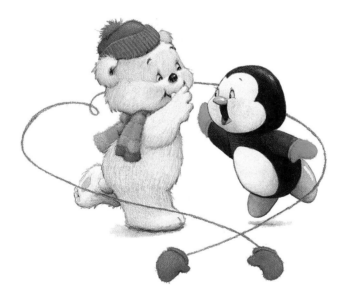

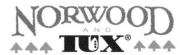

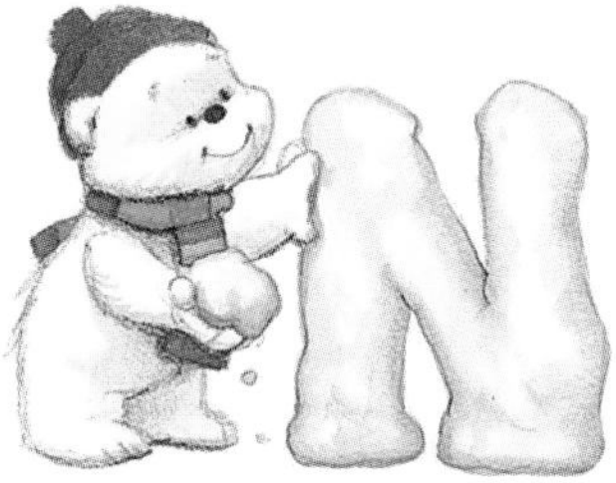

NORWOOD the polar bear awoke one morning, tingling with adventure. He turned to his mother, who was dozing next to him. “Mom,” he whispered, “wake up.”

His mother stirred a bit, made a sputtering sound, then settled back into sleep. Her deep snoring sounded like the motor of a very big snowmobile. “Mom!” Norwood said more earnestly. He gently poked her soft belly with his paw. She kept right on snoring.

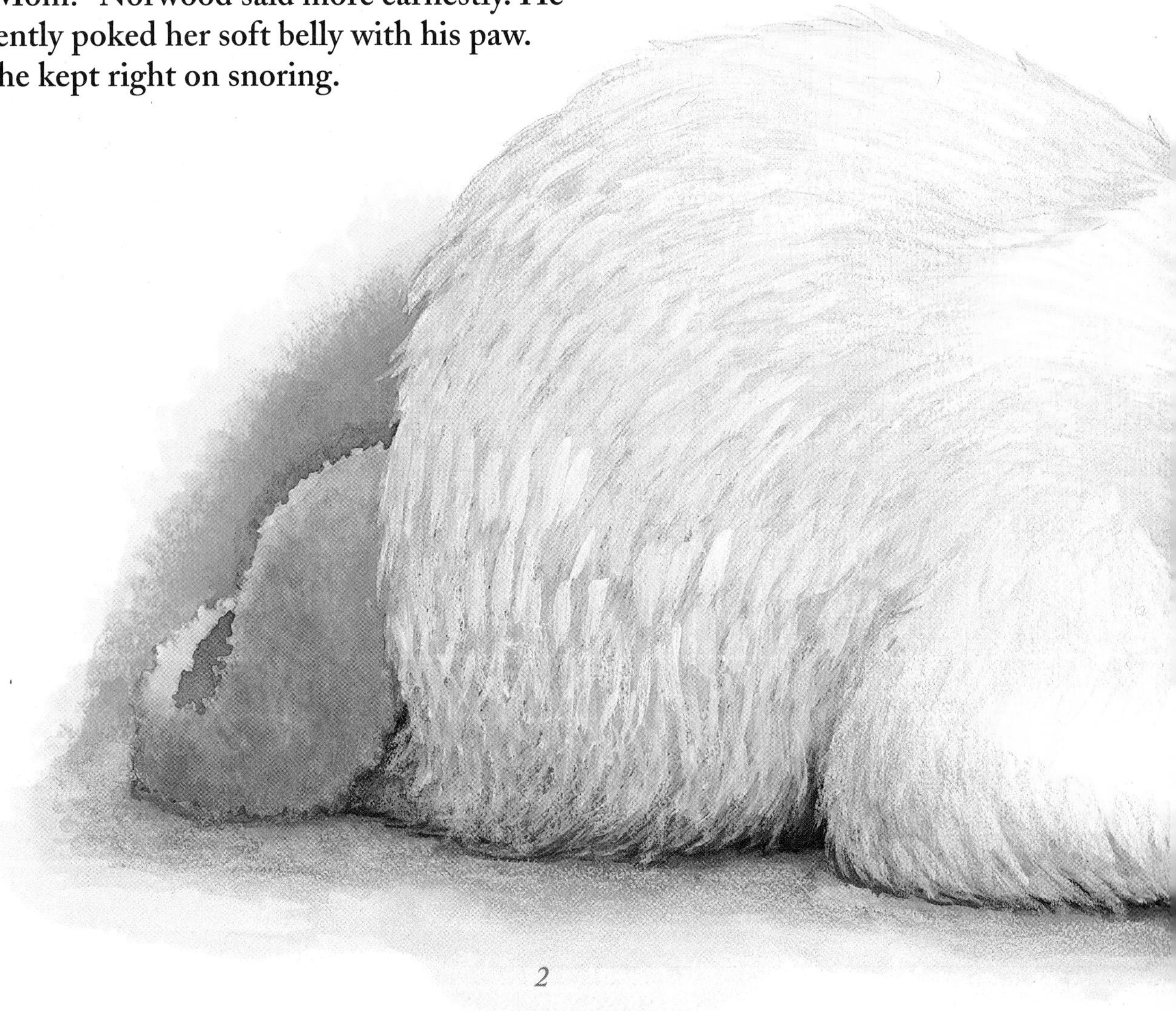

Norwood thoughtfully stroked his chin with his paw. Then he scooped up some fresh North Pole snow and sprinkled it on his mother's nose.

Norwood's mother awoke with a great sneeze. "KACHOO! Why — good morning, Norwood," she said. "Is…is it snowing?"

Norwood giggled. "It was, but it's stopped now."

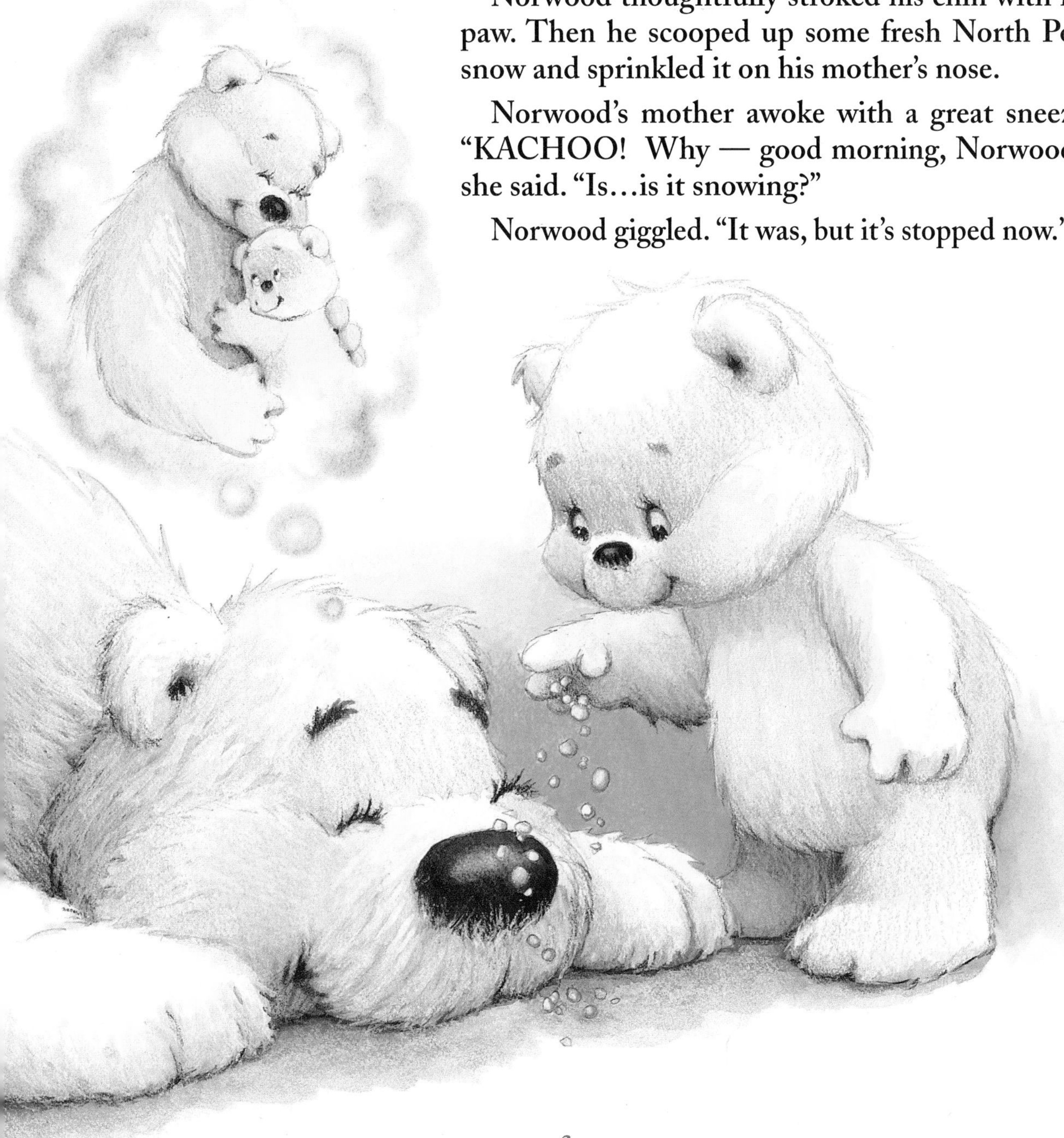

Norwood's mom brushed the snowflakes from her nose. "Let's find some berries for breakfast," she said. "Then we can play."

"Sounds great!" Norwood exclaimed. "Let's have an adventure!"

Norwood's mom smiled. "OK, but if we're going to have an adventure, you better put on your scarf, cap, and…uh-oh!"

"What's wrong, Mom?" Norwood asked.

"I smell something strange," she replied. (She had a superb sniffer, like all polar bears.) "It's not a North Pole smell."

Norwood wrinkled his nose. "You sure it's not Stan the Walrus?"

"I'm sure. Not even Stan the Walrus could smell this bad…look, Norwood! Over there — coming across the ice. Who *are* those creatures?"

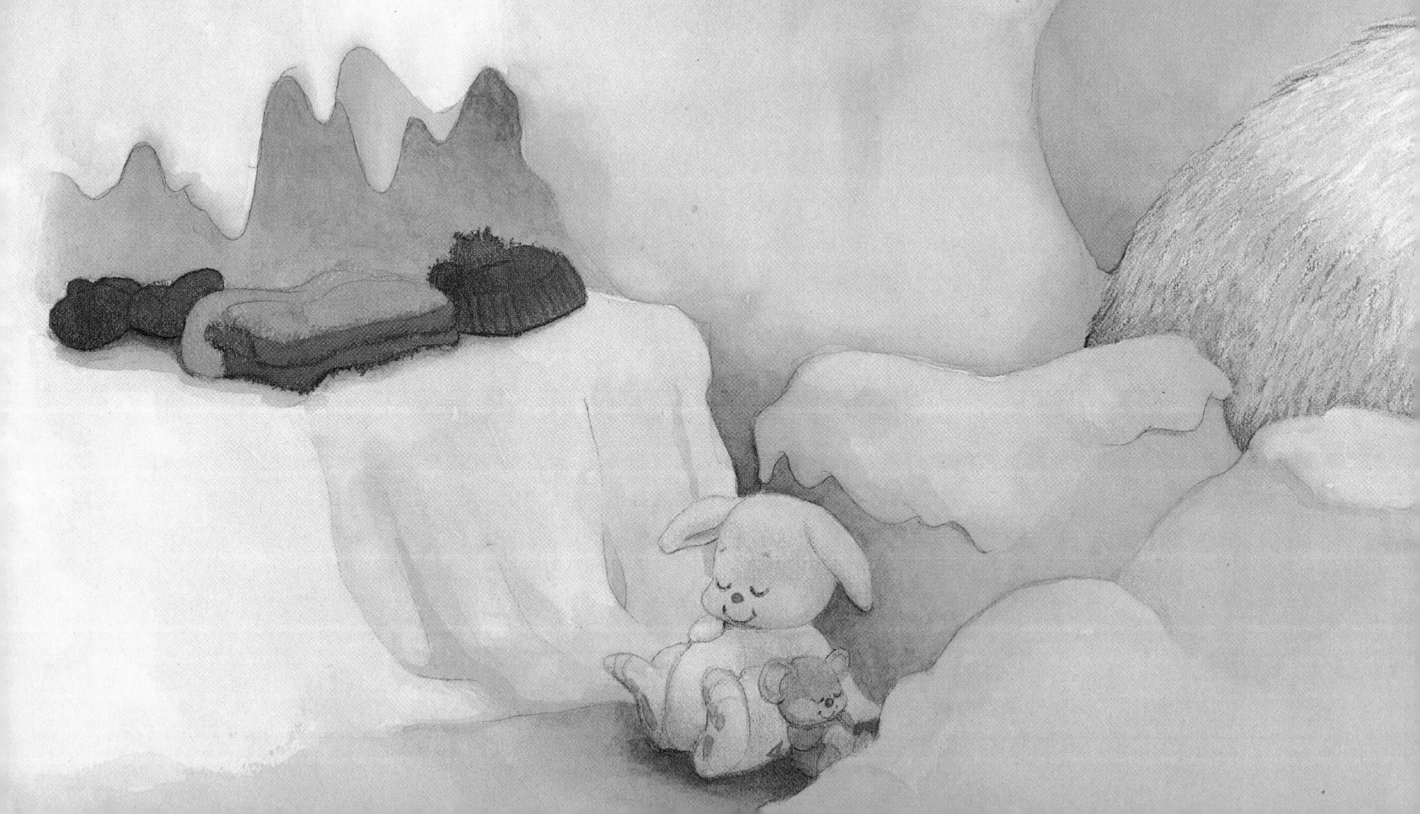

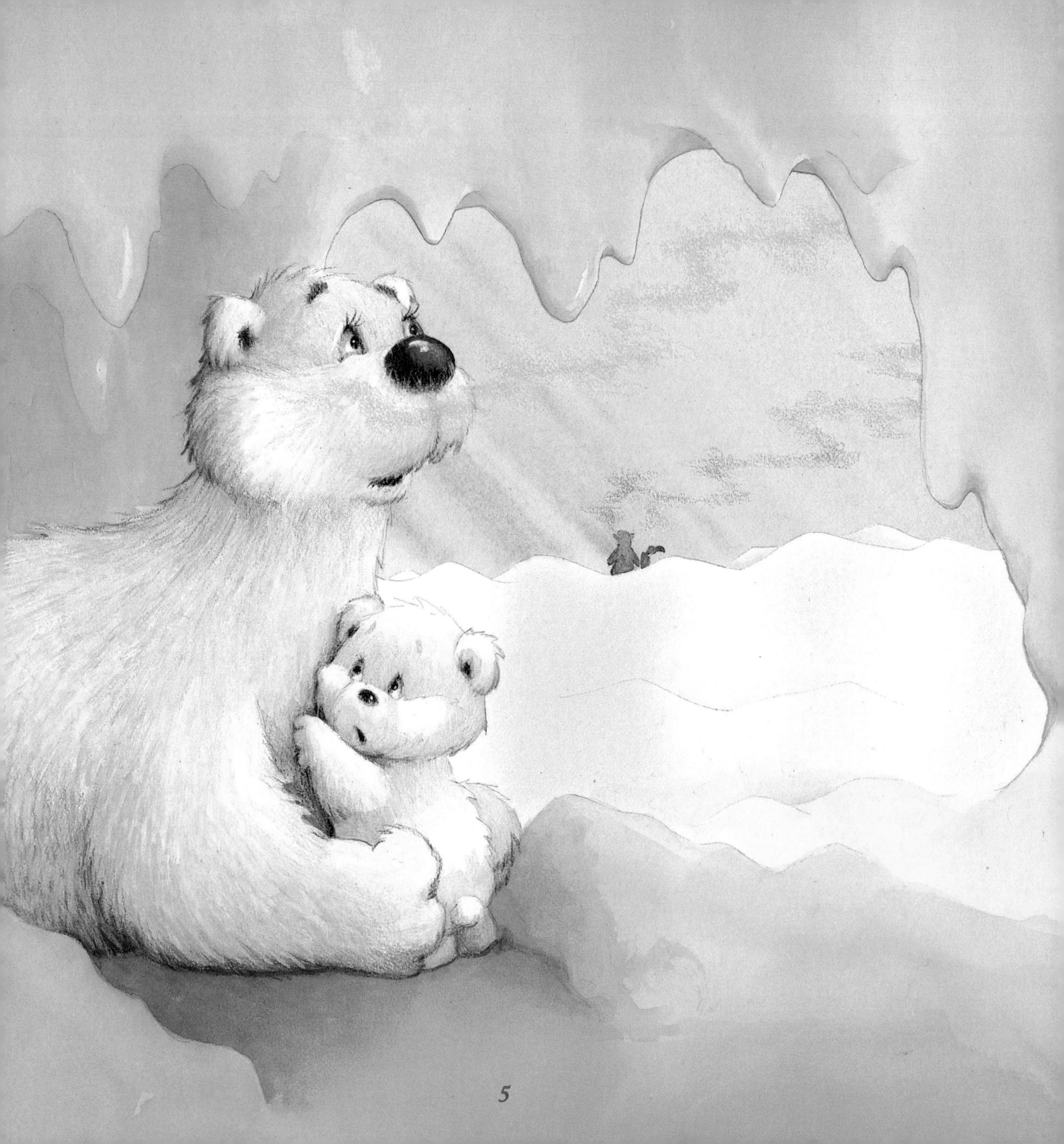

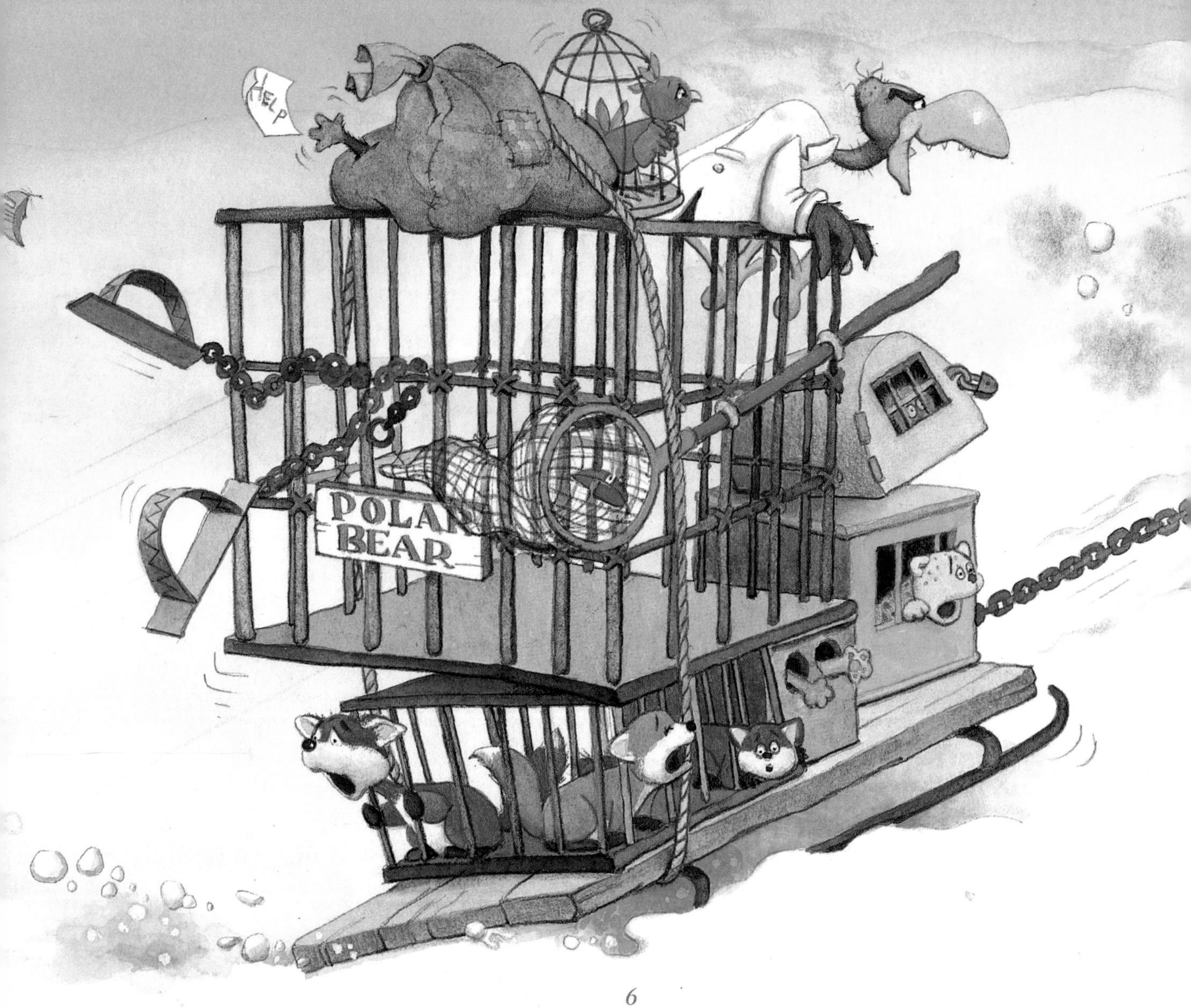
HELP
POLA
BEAR

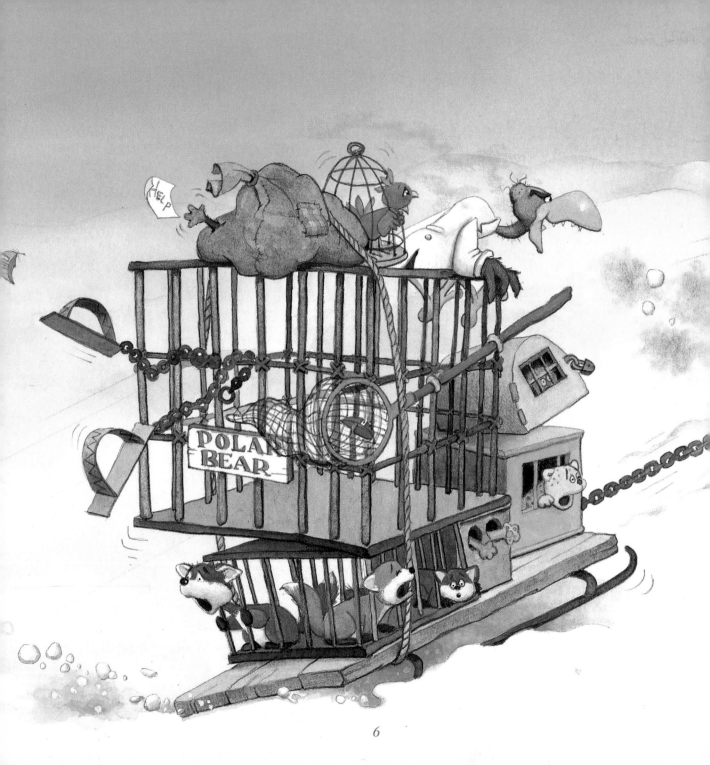

Norwood squinted his chocolate-brown eyes. Then he saw them — a plump man driving a snowmobile and a bald bird sitting on a huge cage.

Norwood's mom put her paws to her face. "Oh, no!" she cried. "I recognize them now. It's Kabloona, the evil trapper, and his partner, Dr. Buzzárd! They must be trapping animals for their traveling zoo! And their zoo is awful, Norwood. It's…it's the wrong sort of zoo!"

"I don't want to be in the wrong sort of zoo, Mom," whimpered Norwood.

"Run!" she commanded.

Norwood began to run with all his might. He glanced over his shoulder. The bird's claws looked as long and sharp as ice picks. And the big man had a snarl on his face and steamy breath billowing from his nostrils and mouth.

Norwood's mother tried to keep up. But her fuzzy pink slippers kept sliding on the ice and snow. (She wore slippers to keep her feet extra warm during North Pole winters.)

As they fled, Norwood realized he and his mother were running out of North Pole. "Mom," he called, "we're coming to the ocean! What do we do?"

"Head for that ice floe over there," she called from behind him.

Norwood skidded to a stop at the edge of the ice. He looked back at his mother. She had fallen in the snow. "Get up, Mom!" he urged. "Come on, pleeeeease!"

But Norwood could see his mother wasn't going to make it. Kabloona and Dr. Buzzárd were closing in. She must have known it too, because as Norwood clambered onto the ice floe, his mother tossed him a pair of mittens. "Take these, Norwood," she called. "They're very special mittens. I've been waiting for the right time to give them to you."

Tears rolled down Norwood's face in slow, sad drips. "Mom, will I see you again?" he sobbed.

"Yes, Norwood, you will, somehow, some way," she replied, with a slight catch in her voice. "Remember, *love is powerful magic!*" Just as she uttered these words, Norwood's mother was covered with a big net.

"Shall I go after the cub?" Norwood heard Dr. Buzzárd ask Kabloona.

"No, we have the mother, Buzzy. Let the runt go."

"Don't call me Buzzy! I'm *Doctor Buzzárd!*" the vulture growled, his beak turning red.

Norwood watched helplessly as they locked his mother in a steel cage. As the ice floe began to carry him from his home, he put his head in his paws and began to cry. A cold wind lashed his face, freezing the tears to his fur. With a deep sigh, he lay down on the floe and closed his eyes.

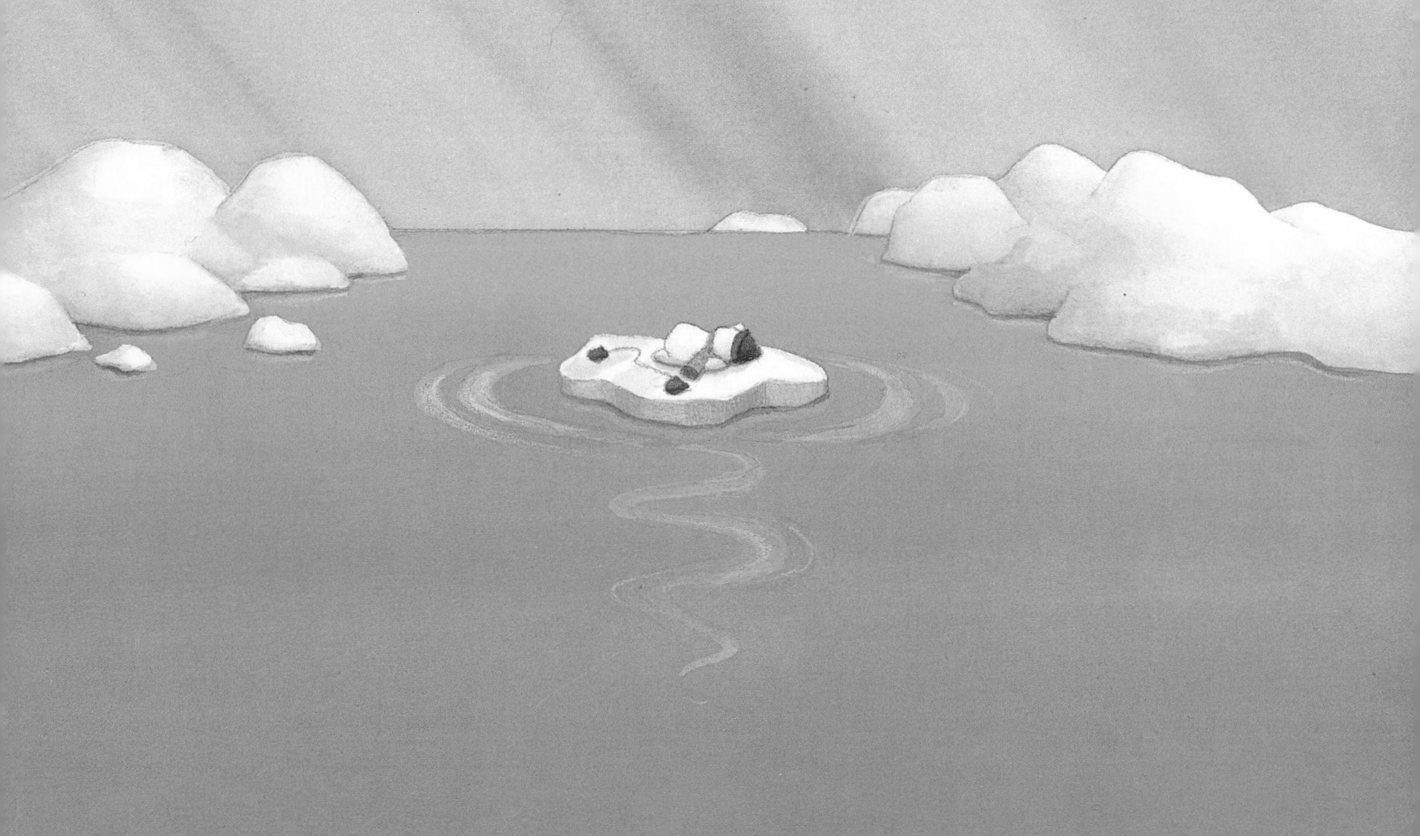

Norwood began to dream. He dreamed and floated for a long time. In one of his dreams, he and his mother were romping across the snow, having snowball fights and building snowbears. Then they stopped to eat some arctic blueberries. As Norwood was enjoying his snack, he heard a faraway call for help.

Norwood awoke for a moment, growled softly, then returned to his dream-berries.

"Help! Help me!"

This time the cry was louder and more urgent. "Who's there?" Norwood asked crossly, his eyes still closed. "I'm eating."

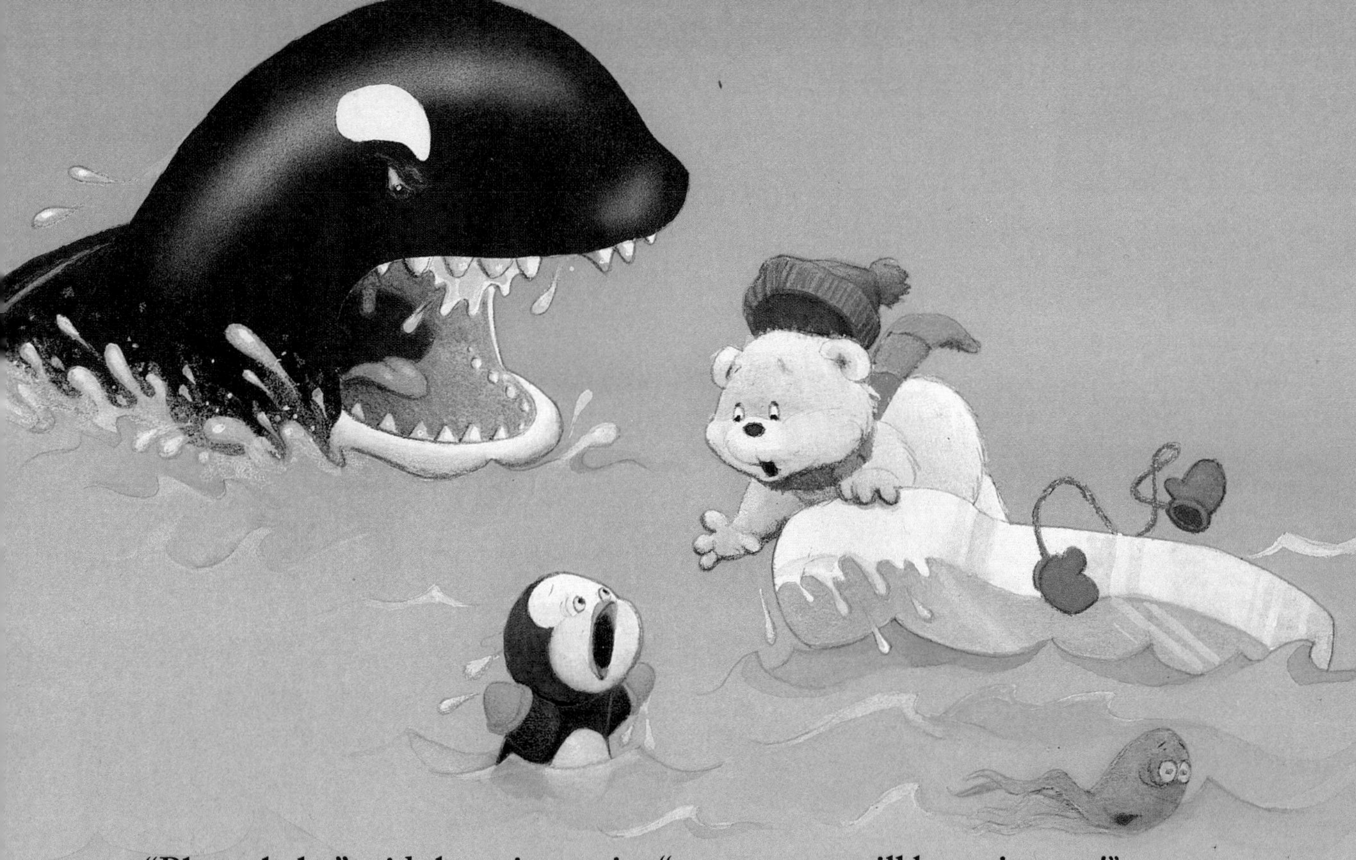

"Please help," said the voice again, "or someone will be eating *me!*"

Norwood opened his eyes. He saw a tiny penguin bobbing in the water near the ice floe. Coming up behind the penguin was the largest killer whale he'd ever seen, its jaws open wide.

"Swim!" urged Norwood. "This way!"

The tiny penguin swam as fast as his flippers could carry him. But the killer whale was catching him. The penguin could feel the whale's hot breath on his tail feathers.

Norwood reached for the penguin and pulled him onto the floe — just as the whale's mouth closed with a great CRACK!

The whale chomped down on the ice floe and gave a loud disappointed groan. Then he swam away, spitting ice and a few broken teeth.

"Great jumpin' jellyfish!" the penguin hollered. "That was close! Thanks!"

Norwood removed his cap, patted down his head fur and straightened his scarf, just as his mother had shown him. "You are most welcome. My name is Norwood," he said, extending his paw.

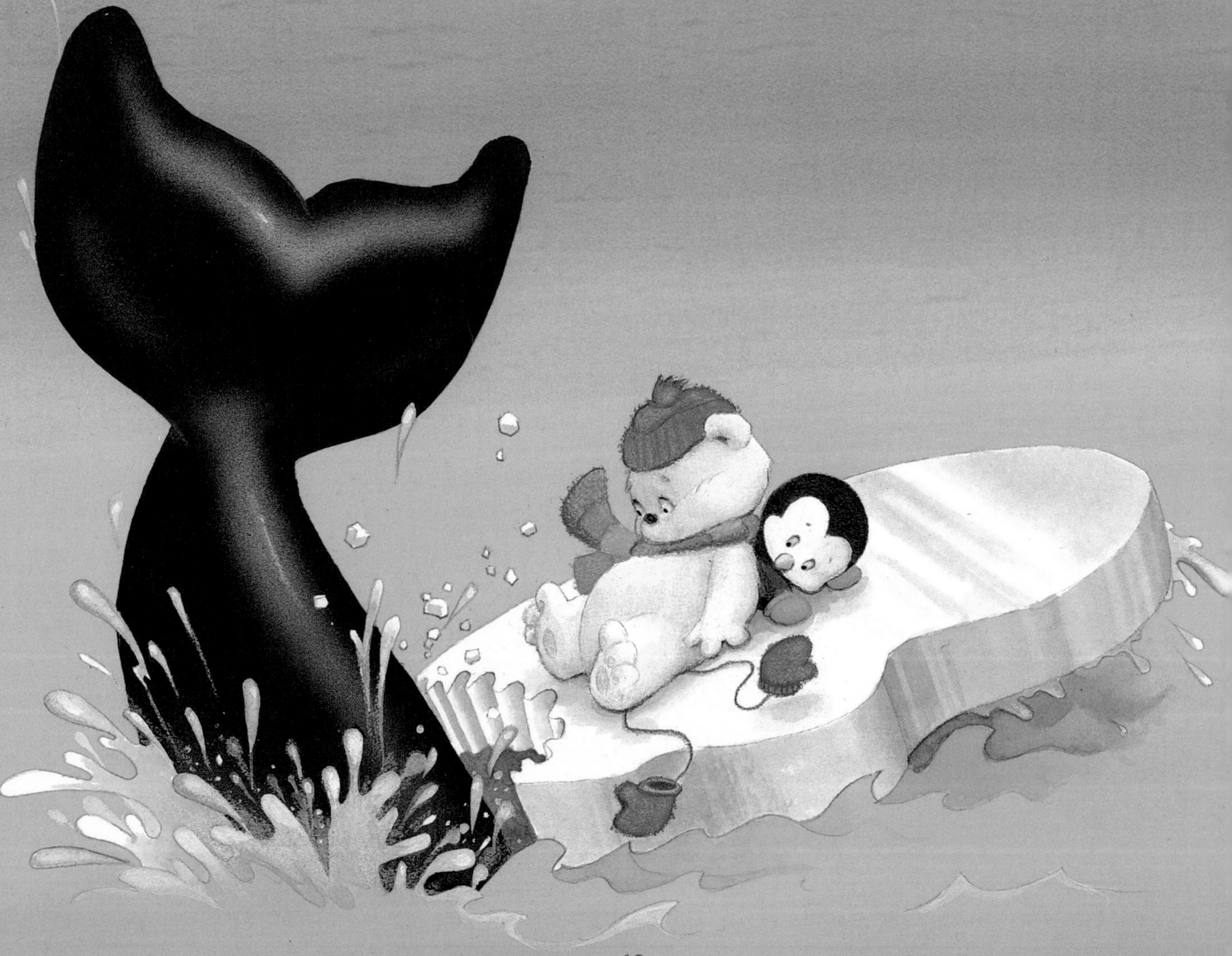

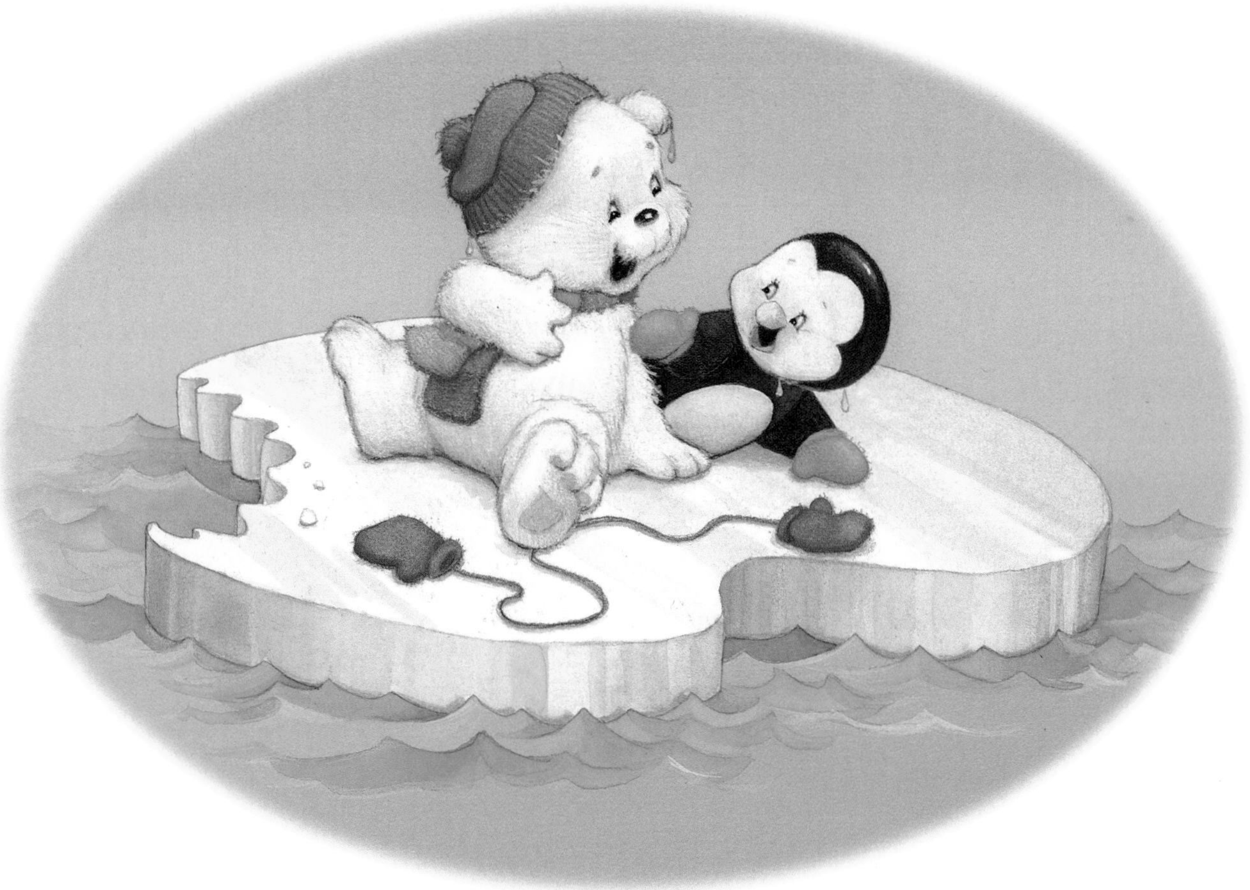

The penguin offered his flipper. “I am Tux. Say, you’re a polar bear, aren’t you?”

“Why, yes. Why do you ask?”

“Because polar bears live at the North Pole, but here you are, all the way at the South Pole!”

“Oh dear,” said Norwood, “I’ve floated to the *wrong* pole. How will I ever find my mom now?”

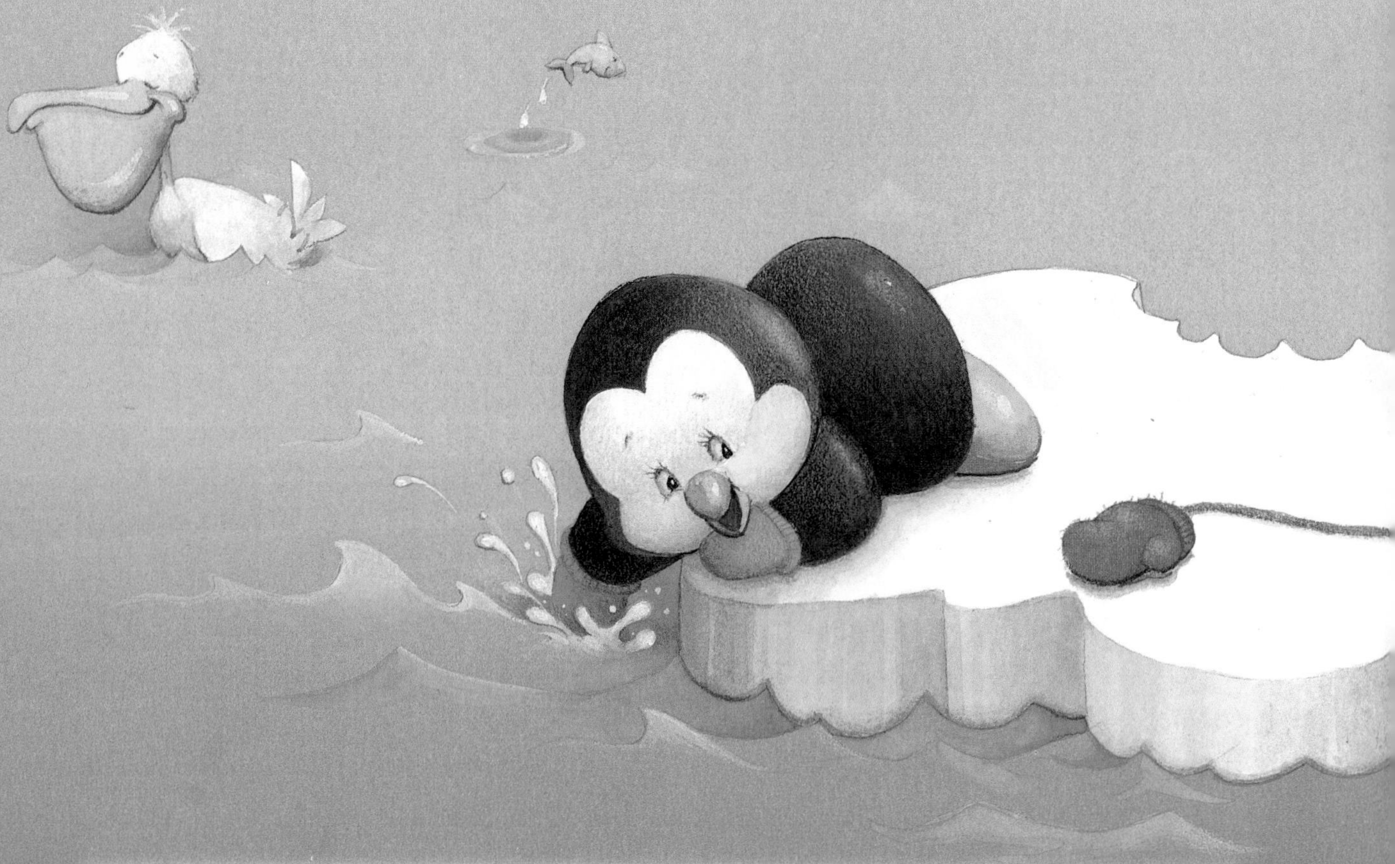

As Norwood examined the bite marks on the ice floe, he told his new friend all about his mother and the devious duo who kidnapped her.

"That's awful," Tux said sincerely. "I've heard of those two. About a year ago, they took my cousin, Reggie Rockhopper Penguin. I'm sorry they got your mother, too. But you'll find her. I could even help you."

"You'd help me?" Norwood asked.

"Sure. I've always wanted to see how the other pole lives. And besides, you saved my life."

"But what will we do?" Norwood asked. "My mom's a whole world away."

Tux thought for a moment. "Well," he said slowly, "if you get on that side of the floe and paddle with your paw, and I paddle on this side with my flipper, we can *paddle* our way to the other pole."

So Norwood and Tux began paddling furiously. After Tux's left flipper and Norwood's right paw began to ache, they traded sides and rowed with all their strength.

15

When Norwood and Tux could paddle no more, they collapsed together on the ice floe, staring up at the night sky. It began to snow. Norwood sat up slowly, opened his mouth and let the snowflakes dance onto his tongue. "That was hard work," he said. "How far do you think we've come?"

Tux flexed his flippers. "About half-way, I guess. Hey, Norwood?"

"Yes."

"I'm cold," Tux said, shivering. "You see, back at the rookery where I live, we penguins all huddle together to stay warm. I guess I'm a little lonely, too. My mom always told me not to swim too far from home, and now I'm lost and it's getting dark and…" Tux began to cry.

Norwood took off his hat. "Here, wear this, Tux. It'll warm you up."

"Thanks," Tux sniffled, taking the hat. He put it on. It covered his head. And his neck. And his shoulders.

"Uh, Norwood," Tux called from under the cap. "I don't think this is going to work."

Norwood lifted the cap off his new friend. Tux smiled a small smile.

Thoughtfully, Norwood put his paw to his mouth, nibbling his mitten. "I've got it!" he shouted.

Norwood removed one of the "very special mittens" his mother had given him. He put it on Tux's head.

"Hey," cried Tux, "this mitten fits me like a glove!"

Norwood and Tux both giggled. But it wasn't long before Tux's giggles turned to sobs again.

"What's wrong, Tux?" Norwood inquired.

"It's just that I'm homesick," Tux said.

"I know the feeling," Norwood said, nodding. "Listen, Tux, you don't have to help me find my mom, if you really don't want to."

"Oh, no," Tux said. "I want to help you. Besides, a promise is a promise. Who knows, maybe we'll find Reggie, too. It's just that... after we find your mom, how will I get back home?" Tux began to cry harder.

Norwood took Tux's face in his furry paws. "Tux, I promise you that my mom and I will help you get back home. It's so nice of you to help me. I'd never leave you stranded. Do you believe me?"

It was now quite dark, but Norwood could feel Tux's head nodding yes. Then he patted Tux on his mitten-covered head. "Don't worry," he said bravely, "as long as we stick together, we'll be OK. As my mom says, *'Love is powerful magic.'*"

No sooner had those words spilled from Norwood's mouth than the ice floe began to glow with a warm, buttery light. Then, the floe slowly and gracefully began to rise from the ocean. Up, up, up it went into the night sky, high above the water. Norwood and Tux stared at the glowing floe, barely daring to believe their eyes.

"N-N-Norwood," Tux said, his beak trembling, "what's happening?"

"I don't know, Tux, but we better not move."

"Norwood, what kind of ice floe is this?"

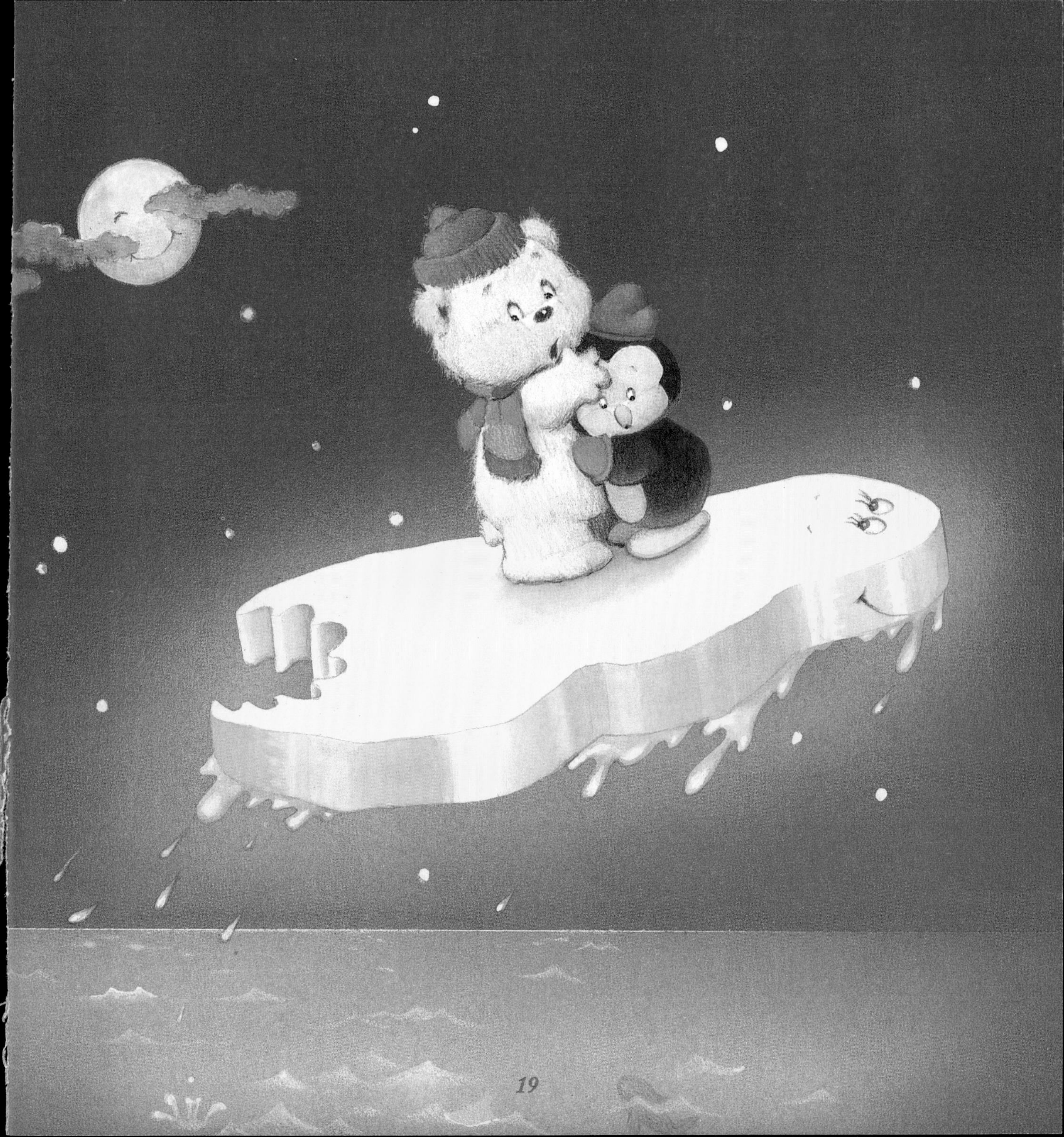

But before Norwood could reply, the ice floe formed a pair of large blue eyes and a wide-smiling mouth and spoke for herself:

"My name is Floe if you must know,
and I'm the only way to go!"

Tux spoke cautiously: "C-C-Could you please go…down?"

Floe said:

"Up or down, I go with the flow.
Where? I really don't care.
East or west —
perhaps to, perhaps fro.
Here is no better than there."

With that, Floe slowly lowered herself back onto the water. But she continued to glow, filling the ocean and the sky above with a light almost as bright as day.

Floe glanced at her stern. "Hmm," she observed,

"I don't wish to seem unrefined,
but whatever happened to my behind?"

"A killer whale did it," Tux said. "I'm sorry."

Floe laughed.

"Oh, well, you know, I really don't mind it.
Heck, I don't care if I ever find it!
A killer whale bite is better than a diet —
I think I'll encourage all my friends to try it!"

"Hey!" Norwood interrupted. "How come you talk in rhymes all the time?"

"The reason that I talk in rhyme?" Floe said. "What better way to pass the time!"

"Cool," replied Norwood.

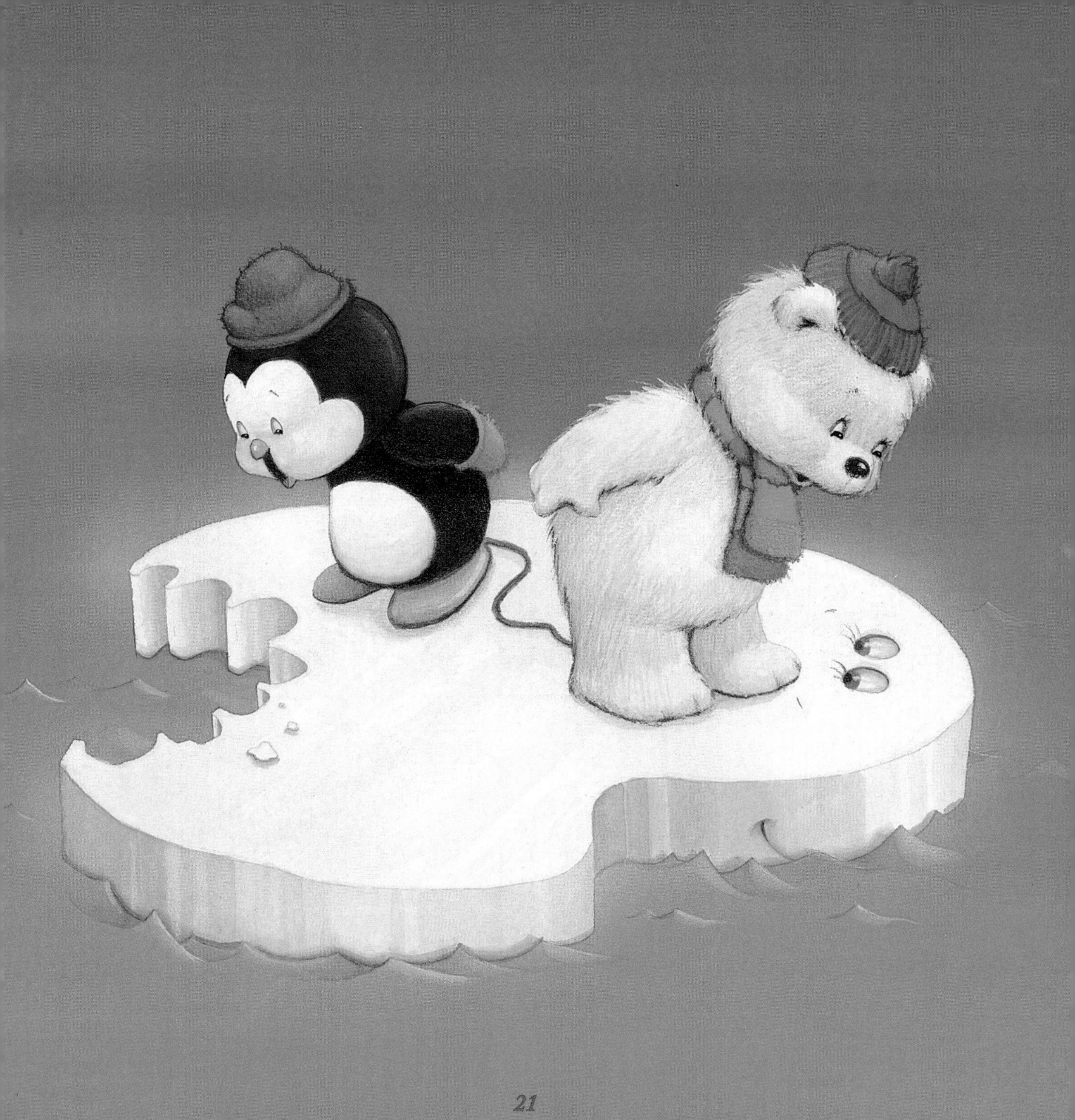

"I still can't believe you're talking at all," said Tux. "I've never heard of a talking ice floe. It must be some kind of magic."

"Magic!" Norwood cried. "Hey, Tux, let's try something. My mom said the mittens she gave me were special, then she said, *'Love is powerful magic.'* Hmm, I wonder."

With that, Norwood placed his mitten on the one Tux was wearing. He cleared his throat, then said solemnly, *"Love is powerful magic."*

The magic worked again. Floe began glowing so brightly that Norwood and Tux had to shield their eyes. "I thought so!" Norwood said excitedly. "The mittens *are* magic. Hey, Tux, wish for something."

Tux thought for a moment. “Well, I wish we had someone to help us rescue –”

In an instant, Norwood saw fish splashing all around Floe, their bodies shining and shimmering in her light.

“Great jumpin’ jellyfish!” Tux shouted. “My ocean friends are here!”

Tux began pointing out his friends to Norwood. “Look! That’s Goldie Prawn and her boyfriend Kurt Mussel. That’s Carp A. Diem and Paul Salmon. And over there is Vince Bluegill with his sidekick Holy Mackerel.”

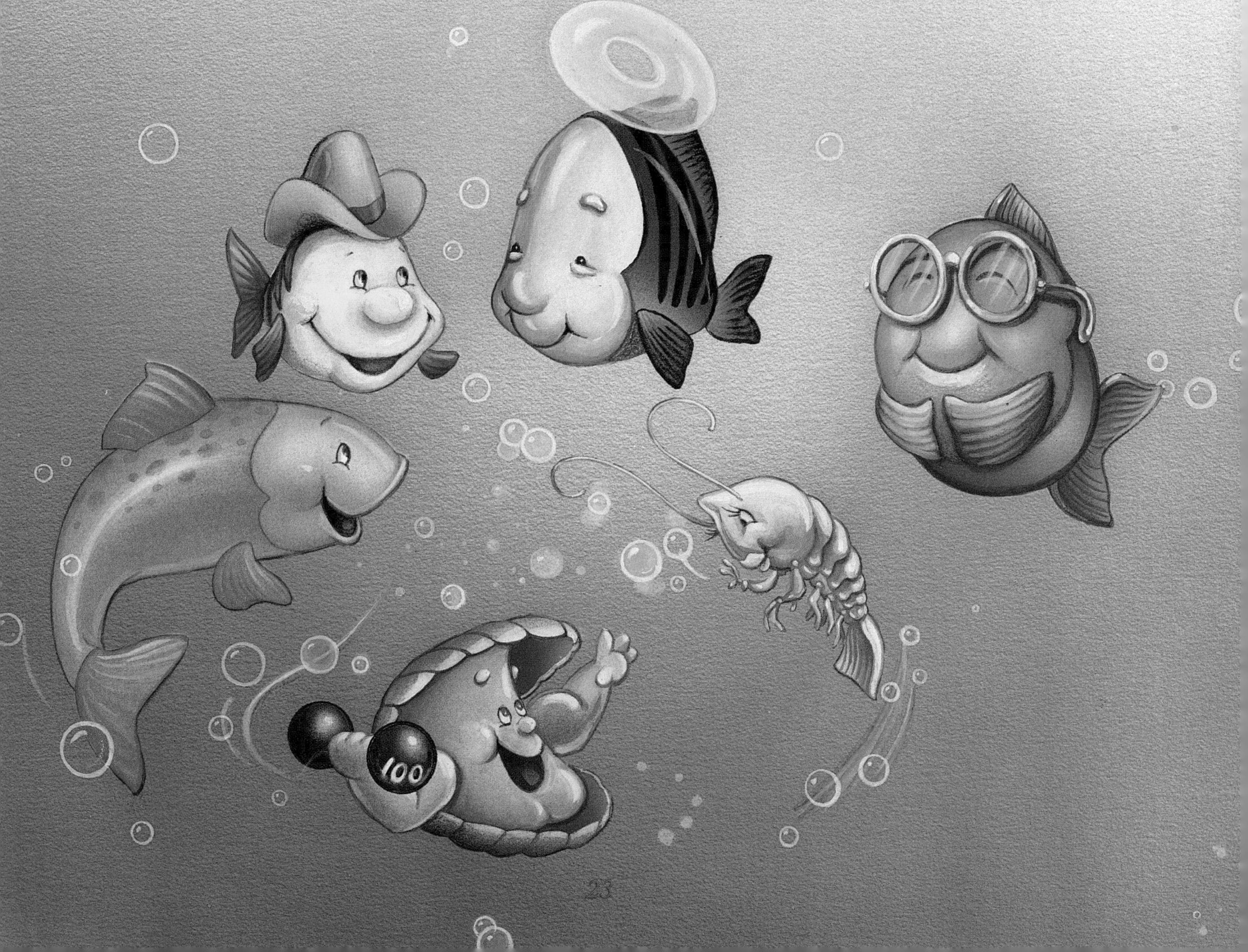
100

After everyone had exchanged hellos, Tux explained Norwood's problem to the fish. "We're so sorry, Norwood," said Goldie Prawn, in a soft, whispery voice. "I wish we could help you find your mother … and your cousin, too, Tux."

Tux addressed his friends: "You *can* help us! You're all a wish-come-true. So, how about it? Are you up for a rescue adventure?"

"Yeah!" they shouted in unison, jumping and splashing in the water.

"In that case," Tux shouted, "it's on to the North Pole. Let's go, Floe!"

As Floe sped toward the North Pole, Norwood tingled with excitement, just as he had the morning he lost his mother. After all, he now had a pair of magic mittens, a talking and flying ice floe, and a host of new friends—including a new *best* friend. Best of all, in his heart he knew that very soon he would have his mother again, too.

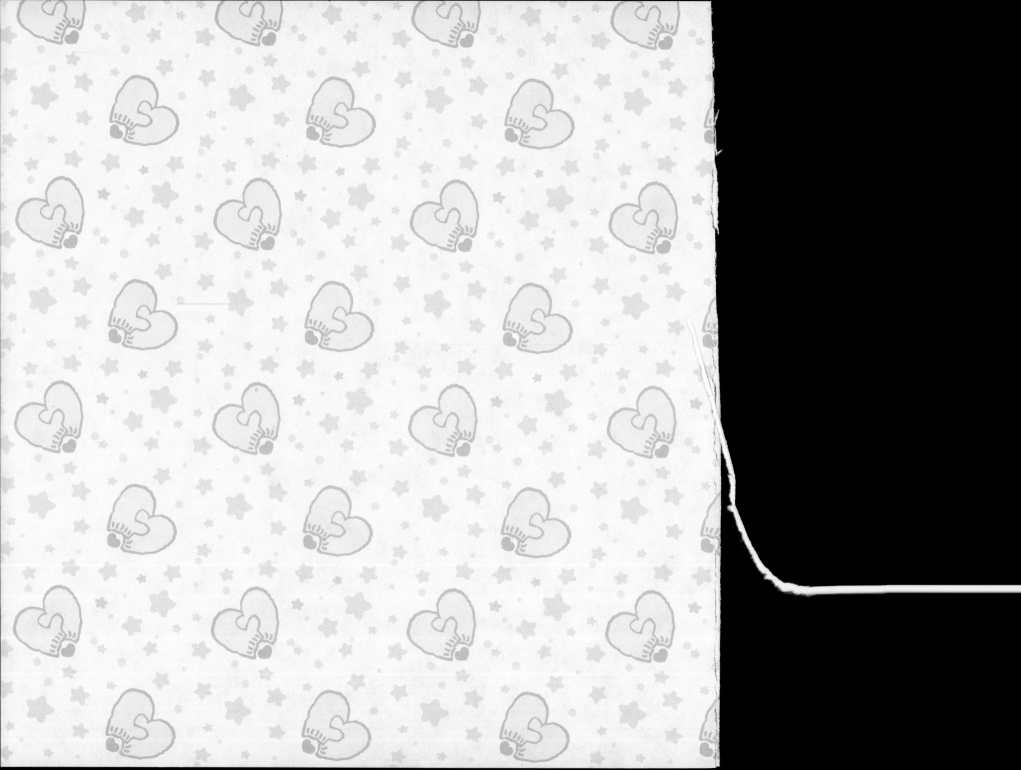